Beach play

by Marsha Hayles • illustrated by Hideko Takahashi

Henry Holt and Company • New York

Beach day playing
Sunning
Shading

Playground romping
Ocean wading.

Smacking
Packing
Sandy
Stacking

Splashing
Dashing

Big wave crashing.

Blanket spreading
Picnic lunching

Sandwiches made for
Beachy munching.

Climbing
Dangling
Body tangling

Hands go slipping
Down
Zoom
Zipping.

Perching

Springing

Flying

Swinging

Braking, slowing

Bare-toe hoeing.

Ice cream licking

Drippy

Sticking

ICE CREAM

VANILLA

STRAWBERRY

CHOCOLATE

MINT CHOCOLATE CHIP

Arching

Stretching

Frisbee catching.

Salty swimming
Wavy floating

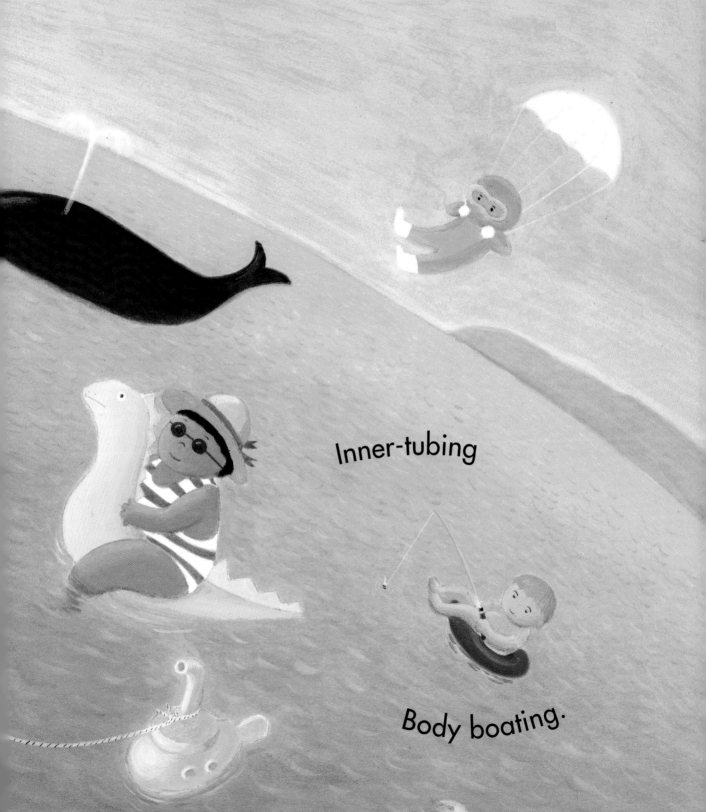

Inner-tubing

Body boating.

Sunlight fading

Cool breeze blowing

Wrapping up now
Time for going.

Blankets, towels
Held for shaking

Ocean treasures
Held for taking.

Backseat nesting
Ocean gleaming

Seaside resting
Beach day dreaming.

To Mayme and Al, who made my own
childhood full of love and play —M.H.

To Obâchan (my grandmother) —H.T.

Henry Holt and Company, Inc.
Publishers since 1866
115 West 18th Street
New York, New York 10011

Henry Holt is a registered trademark of
Henry Holt and Company, Inc.

Text copyright © 1998 by Marsha Hayles
Illustrations copyright © 1998 by Hideko Takahashi
All rights reserved.
Published in Canada by Fitzhenry & Whiteside Ltd.,
195 Allstate Parkway, Markham, Ontario L3R 4T8.

Library of Congress Cataloging-in-Publication Data
Hayles, Marsha.
  Beach play / by Marsha Hayles; illustrated by Hideko Takahashi.
Summary: The sunny beach offers many fun and exciting activities for
those who spend a day playing on its warm sands and in the water.
  [1. Beaches—Fiction. 2. Play—Fiction. 3. Day—Fiction. 4. Stories in
rhyme.] I. Takahashi, Hideko, ill. II. Title. PZ8.3.H326Bh
1997 [E]—dc21   97-16086

ISBN 0-8050-4271-7
First Edition—1998
Designed by Meredith Baldwin
The artist used acrylic on illustration board to create
the illustrations for this book.

Printed in the United States of America on acid-free paper.∞
10 9 8 7 6 5 4 3 2 1